Friends Solve Problems

Metro Early Reading Program

Level F, Stories 1–5

Credits
Illustration: Front cover, Pat Paris
Photography: Front and back covers, (Atlanta, Georgia) Greg Probst/Stone

ISBN 1-58120-624-0

1 2 3 4 5 6 7 8 9 CL 03 02 01 00

Table of Contents

Pen Pals

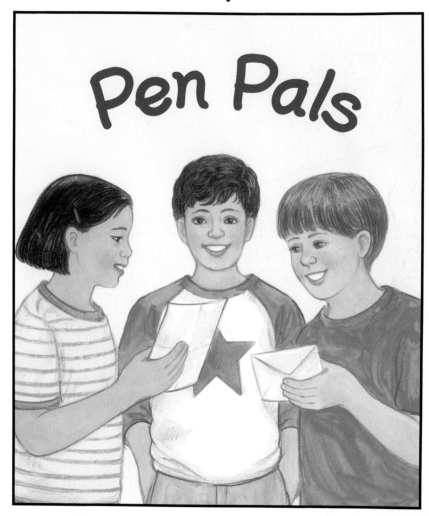

Mr. West walked to the board. He wrote <u>Pen Pals</u> in big letters. "Can any of you tell me what a pen pal is?" he asked.

"I know," said Jed. "A pen pal is a person you send letters to. A pen pal can be far away. You may never even meet your pen pal."

"You send pictures and cards to your pen pal," said Ravi. "You tell your pen pal about your friends and the kinds of things you like to do. It's fun to write and to get letters back."

"That's right," said Mr. West. "You'll find out how you and your pen pal are different. You'll also find out how you're the same. You may even get to be true friends." Mr. West had a stack of cards. Each one had a name on it. He gave a card to each person in his class.

"Start by planning what you'd like to write," said Mr. West. "Take out a sheet of blank paper. Think about things you'd like to tell your pen pal. Make a list. Keep adding things as you think of them. Then pick a few things and rewrite them in a letter."

Dan's pen pal was named Mark. Dan wanted to write to him, but he could think of nothing to say. "This is the hardest job," thought Dan. "I'll bet Mark does lots of fun things. I never do any fun things."

"I don't know where to start," said Dan. "This is a harder job than other homework."

"It's not so hard. Just write down what you like to do," said Lin. "Beth is my pen pal. I'm going to send her a card with a yellow flower on it. I'll write about Patches."

That night Dan worked hard on his letter. Still, he didn't think that it was any good. "This is the hardest homework," Dan said to Sara. "I don't know what to write to Mark."

"He'd like to read about the cool plane you made with Jamal," said Sara. "He'd want to know how you learned to use a camera."

"The plane was not that great," said Dan. "Lots of kids know how to use a camera. That's nothing. I would like to write about something different. I wish I had an adventure to write about. I could make up a story for Mark. Then he'd think I was the coolest kid."

"You're the coolest kid now," said Sara. "You write so well. You don't have to tell a story that isn't true. That would be wrong."

"You're right, Sara," said Dan. "I need to think some more about what to write."

The next day the class talked about writing to their pen pals.

"I drew yellow flowers on my card for Beth. I drew a picture of my house and Patches. This is what I wrote," said Lin.

"Dear Beth, My name is Lin. This is the house I share with my mother, grandfather, and grandmother. My friends and I do many different things. We make clay animals. We take pictures with cameras. I wanted a dog for the longest time. Now I have Patches. I drew a picture of him for you. What kinds of things do you like to do? Write soon. Your pal, Lin."

"You draw so well, Lin," said Mr. West. "I like these yellow flowers. Good job. Who would like to go next?"

"This was a harder letter to write than I thought it would be," said Dan. "I had to redo it two times. Here it is."

9

"Dear Mark, My name is Dan. I wanted to write about making a plane with Jamal or about camping with Jed. I wanted to write about the day Ben's dog, Mop, went for a swim with us. But I didn't think these were very good adventures. I'd like to write a longer letter, but I can't think of what to write. Please write back to me soon. From Dan."

"What you wrote is just not true," said Jed. "There's nothing wrong with our adventures. We have had some fun times."

"Your letter doesn't tell about what kind of person you are," said Mr. West. "Mark won't get to know you from that letter. Think of something you'd like to tell Mark about the things you do. I'd like you to rewrite the letter."

11

Lin and Jed went to talk to Dan. "I have to redo this letter," said Dan.

"We'll help you redo it," said Lin.

"Three heads are better than one," said Jed. "You can rewrite the letter with our help."

Lin got out a blank sheet of paper. "First, what could you write about?" she asked.

"What about when we made a house for Patches and he didn't fit inside?" asked Jed.

"You can write about going camping with Jed and his dad," said Lin. "And about the tent."

"The tent had big rips in it," said Dan. "We were cold and wet. But we still had some fun. The pancakes were great."

"See? You do have things to write about," said Jed.

A few weeks went by. One day Mr. West wrote some names on the board. "These are the pen pals who wrote back so far," he said. "I'll pass their letters out. You can read them and share them with the class if you like."

Ken
Mark
Beth
Josh
Ana
Kate
Nick

Dan saw Mark's name on the board. He took the letter and read it. "Why don't you read Mark's letter to the class?" said Mr. West.

"This is what Mark wrote," said Dan. "Dear Dan, Your story about camping made me laugh. I laughed so hard I couldn't stand up. I like camping, too. My dad and I have a tent, but it doesn't have any rips. I'd like to have the same kind of adventures you have. Write a longer letter soon. I want to laugh some more. Your pal, Mark."

"That's a great letter," said Lin. "You and Mark make good pen pals."

"I thought having a pen pal was hard," said Dan. "But I was wrong. I have so much to tell Mark. I'm going to write the longest letter!"

Dan took out a blank sheet of paper and got started.

The Horse Show

Tasha had been playing with her gray pony all morning. She brushed it. She made it run around the ring. She turned it one way and then the other. She liked playing with her little gray pony.

"You have been playing with that little horse all morning," said Ben. "Aren't you sick of it yet?"

"It's a pony, not a horse," said Tasha. "I never get sick of it. I have a smaller pony, too. Do you want to play with a brown pony?"

"No way!" said Ben.

"You don't have to hurt the pony's feelings!" said Tasha. "I know something that you don't know. Mom is taking us downtown. We're all going to go to a horse show together. I need to go look for my cowgirl outfit."

Tasha was looking in her closet when Mom came into the room. "Tasha, get dressed," said Mom. "We just have a short time to get downtown."

"I want to put on my cowgirl outfit," said Tasha. "I've only worn it once before. It will be just right for the horse show."

"Do you think your outfit still fits?" asked Mom. "I hope it's not too short."

"It won't be too short," said Tasha. "I'll put on my cowgirl hat, too. I know that's not too small. I've worn it a lot."

"Where are my cowgirl boots?" asked Tasha. Mom looked in Tasha's closet. "Here are your boots," she said. "Try them on. You have not worn these boots in a long time. I hope they don't hurt your feet. Dress quickly now."

"What a sister!" Ben said. "Where is she? If she doesn't come out soon we'll miss the show. Tasha is the one who likes horses, and she's taking the longest time!"

"We can get downtown quickly," said Mom. "We won't be late."

Just then Tasha came into the room. "You
look just like a cowgirl, Tasha," said Mom.
"Turn around." Tasha turned around so Mom
and Ben could see her outfit.

"Too bad you don't have a horse," Ben said.

"I'll ride a horse at the show," said Tasha.

"Don't feel bad, but you won't ride," said
Ben. "We're just going to see the show."

"What? I don't want to just look. I want to be
in the horse show," said Tasha.

There was a big crowd at the horse show. Cowboys and cowgirls were riding beautiful horses around the ring. Some horses were doing jumps.

"It just isn't right," said Tasha. "Look at all the horses. I want to ride one. That smaller horse looks just like my brown pony."

"Don't feel bad, Tasha," said Ben. "This show is great. It's better than I thought it would be. The horses and riders can do many different tricks. I'm glad that I came."

"The crowd shouted loudly when the cowgirl on the gray horse went by," said Mom. "She and her horse can do a lot of tricks."

"If I had a horse I'd be in the show," said Tasha. "The crowd would shout loudly for me."

"That was the best cowgirl," said Ben. "The gray horse she was on did the greatest tricks. She might get to be queen of the show."

"I can't wait to see what will be next," said Tasha. "I want to see more tricks."

More cowboys came riding out on their horses. They went around the ring quickly. One cowboy had a beautiful black horse. The cowboy made his horse bow for the crowd.

"I've never seen a horse bow before," said Ben. "That's something new."

"That horse does so many tricks," said Tasha. "Did you see it jump over the bench? I've never seen that before. That cowboy will be king of the show. I wish I could be the queen."

   At the end of the show, one cowboy in a
brown hat came out into the ring. "We've seen
a lot of talent," he said. "You all shouted loudly
when you saw the tricks these horses and riders
could do. Lee was the rider on the black horse.
Jean was the rider on the gray horse. Jean
and Lee have been picked as king and queen
of the horse show!"
   "The crowd is shouting for Jean and Lee,"
said Mom. "Now they'll ride around the ring
together as the king and queen."

"We have a pony wagon," said the cowboy in the ring. "We've put the names of all the kids in the crowd in this hat. I'll draw names out of the hat. If I say your name, come down quickly and get in the wagon. You can all ride around together with the king and queen."

The cowboy started calling names. He called Ben's name. Ben ran down to the wagon.

"I hope he calls my name," said Tasha.

"He may call your name, Tasha," said Mom. "He's drawing some more names now."

The cowboy called some more names. Soon there was no more room in the wagon. Tasha would not get to ride around the ring. She was sad.

"What is Ben doing?" said Mom. "He's talking to that cowboy. What is he saying?"

"A boy in the wagon said he'd give his place to his sister," said the cowboy. "But we've got a better place for her. We need a little cowgirl to ride on the pony. So, Tasha, Ben's sister, come on down."

"You're the greatest friend, Ben," said Tasha.
"That was very nice of you, Ben," said Mom.
"I know, Mom," said Ben. "Tasha's feelings would have been hurt if she couldn't ride in the ring. Now she'll be talking for days about how she got to ride in the horse show."

Carlos looked at his plate. He wanted to eat, but he had something to say. "Mr. Sterling wants to give me a job at his pizza shop," he said. "I can work there after school. May I do it?"

"What would you do there?" asked Papa.

"Mr. Sterling said he'd teach me how to make pizza," said Carlos. "I'd make the dough and the sauce, and I'd help clean up. I'd slice up the pizza and serve it."

"That sounds good," said Mama. "But I think Mr. Sterling made a mistake. Does he know how much you like to eat pizza?"

"Come on, Mama," said Carlos. "I like pizza, but I'll leave some for the shop!"

The next day, Carlos went to The Pizza Pie after school. Mr. Sterling was waiting for him. He gave Carlos a shirt with the name of the shop on it. "Making pizza is going to be a big part of your job, Carlos," he said. "I'll show you how to do it. First, let's clean our hands."

"Yes, sir," said Carlos. "What's next?"

"I have the dough right here," said Mr. Sterling. "But we have to roll it out."

Next, Mr. Sterling showed Carlos how to roll and stretch the dough. Then he put it on a big pizza pan. "Now, the fun part," said Mr. Sterling. "We put on sauce, cheese, and toppings. Go on, Carlos. You try it. You're doing very well."

Mr. Sterling showed Carlos how to open the oven and put in the pizza. "We have to check the pie so it doesn't burn," he said. "Let's start cleaning up. How strange."

"What's strange?" asked Carlos.

"My gold ring," said Mr. Sterling. "I had it on before. Did I misplace it? I'll see if I left it in the back. Can you look after the shop?"

"Yes, sir!" said Carlos. "If people come, I'll serve them a slice of the best pizza ever."

In a little while, two boys came into the shop. They were friends from school. "We'll take two slices each," Nick said.

"I didn't know you worked here," Omar said.

"It's my first day," said Carlos. "It's a cool job so far."

"How can I get a shirt like that?" asked Nick.

"You have to get a job here first," said Carlos.

Nick and Omar ate their pizza quickly. "That pizza was so good it should win a prize," Omar said. "But we have to go now, Carlos."

"We'll see you at school," said Nick.

Next, Marta and Papa came to see how Carlos was doing at his new job. "Two slices of pizza, please," said Papa.

"Yes, sir. Two hot slices, coming up," said Carlos. "Eat them before they get cold."

"I like your Pizza Pie shirt," said Marta.

"Thanks," said Carlos. "Mr. Sterling gave it to me. He's in the back looking for the ring he misplaced."

"He misplaced his ring?" asked Papa. "Maybe we can help look for it."

"Tell us what you have learned," Papa said.

"I helped Mr. Sterling make pizza," said Carlos. "I helped roll out the dough, and then I put sauce and cheese and some toppings on it. Now, I'm a lean, mean pizza machine."

"I should make another pizza," Carlos said.
"My friends from school can sure eat!"

Carlos started to roll out the dough. "I think
you made a mistake, Carlos," said Marta. "That
doesn't look much like pizza to me."

"There's no mistake," said Carlos. "I just have
to stretch the dough until it fills the pan."

"I'm not so sure you know what you're doing,
Carlos," said Marta.

"I'm sure," said Carlos. "I'm the lean, mean
pizza machine."

"You saw me roll out the dough and put it in the pan," said Carlos. "Now comes the fun part. First, I put on sauce and cheese, and then all these other toppings. When it's done, this will be the best pizza pie ever. You'll see."

Mr. Sterling came back. "Strange," he said. "I can't find that gold ring."

"We looked for it out here," said Marta. "But we couldn't find it."

"Maybe it will turn up," said Mr. Sterling. "Let's get back to work, Carlos."

Papa and Marta looked at the pizza Carlos had made. It had lots of stuff on it. "I hope that pizza turns out all right," said Papa.

"Be cool, Papa," said Carlos. "I know what I'm doing. I'm a lean, mean pizza machine."

"Your dad is right," said Mr. Sterling. "I've never seen so much stuff on a pizza before! But it doesn't look bad. It looks very good. Let's get it into the oven. We'll see how it turns out when it's done."

"I'll check the pizza so it doesn't burn," said Carlos. "Then we can serve it up."

"Good, Carlos," said Mr. Sterling. "You're learning fast. You'll be opening your own pizza shop before you know it."

Carlos opened the oven. "It's done," said Carlos. "The best pizza ever. It didn't burn. It turned out great!"

"What a pizza," said Papa. "Look at all that good stuff on it. But what's shining on the pizza there?" He showed them a lump.

"It's my ring!" said Mr. Sterling. "It must have come off when I mixed the dough. Good work, Carlos. You're a true prize."

"And you baked a prize into your pizza, too," said Marta. "Maybe you are a lean, mean pizza machine, after all."

The School Band

One day, Mr. Sanchez, the music teacher, came to talk to the class. He needed boys and girls to play in the school band. "We have fun in the band," he said. "If you join, you'll play with other kids and learn many songs."

"I think I'd like to join the school band," said Jed. "Maybe I'd like to play the sax. Is it hard to play a sax?"

"It's not a matter of hard," said Mr. Sanchez. "It's a matter of work. The kids in the band play every single night, and after school, too."

"That sounds hard," said Jed.

"It might be hard, but you can handle it. No pain, no gain. That's what I tell the boys and girls in the band," said Mr. Sanchez.

On the way home, the kids talked about the band. "I might try to learn to play the flute," said Dan. "But it sounds like a lot of work. We would have to play music every night."

"I could handle that," said Lin. "I like music. I'd like to learn to play the flute. Mr. Sanchez said the kids have a lot of fun. So what if we have to play every night? No pain, no gain."

"I want to join the band, too," said Jed. "But what if we don't sound good?"

"We won't sound that bad," said Lin. "Mr. Sanchez will give us lessons. We'll have fun."

"You talked me into it, Lin," said Dan.

"It's all set," said Jed. "Soon we'll all be playing in the band."

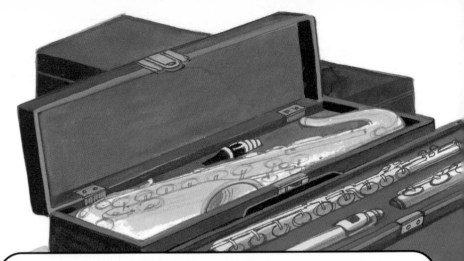

A few days later, Lin, Jed, and Dan went to the band room for their first lesson. Mr. Sanchez was there waiting for them. He took a sax from one box and handed it to Jed. He gave the flutes to Lin and Dan.

"I'll work with each of you to get you started," Mr. Sanchez said to them. "Then I want you to work at home on what I show you. You won't start right away with the band. It will be four weeks before you do. Until then, I'll give you each lessons."

"But we can't play a single note," said Dan.

"That doesn't matter. You'll learn," said Mr. Sanchez. "Work at home each night. If you do, you'll get better. Learning to play music takes time."

After the lesson, the three friends went to Dan's house to play. Lin took her flute and tried to blow softly into it.

"What a strange noise!" said Jed. "You made a squeak. It didn't sound like music at all."

"That sounded very, very bad," said Lin.

"I'm going to try the sax," said Jed. "I won't blow softly. I'll blow as hard as I can."

"That was a squeal," said Dan. "Once I had a toy sax, but it never made a noise that bad."

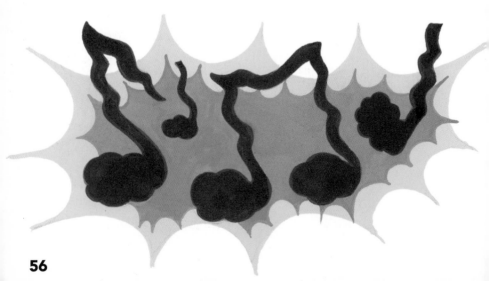

"I did my best," said Jed. "You should try."

"Mr. Sanchez said that learning to play music takes time," said Lin. "He wants us to start with the band in four weeks. Let's keep trying. I'm sure we'll be better by then."

Four weeks later, the three friends talked on their way to school. It was going to be their first day playing with the band. Now they were not sure they wanted to do it. "I've tried to do what Mr. Sanchez told me," said Lin. "But all that comes out is an annoying squeal."

"I made a lot of squeaks and squeals last night," said Dan. "But Sara and Nina liked it. They laughed so hard their sides hurt."

"I've played my sax a lot," said Jed. "I made a lot of noise. Grandmother said it was starting to annoy her. It even started to annoy me. I have to think this over. I want to be in the band. I knew it would take work, but I don't want to sound so bad."

After school the three friends went to talk to Mr. Sanchez. They were scared about playing with the band. They wanted to do well.

"I work on the songs every single night," said Lin. "I blow softly, but the sound that comes out is so bad."

"When it comes to playing the flute, I stink," said Dan.

"My music sounds like squeaks," said Jed. "I knew it would take time, but I'm still so bad."

"Wait," said Mr. Sanchez. "You just started. I'll show you how quickly things can change. I made a tape the first day the band met. Here it is. I'll play it for you. Then you can tell me what you think."

"The band sounds so bad in that tape," said Jed. "Their playing is as bad as mine."

"Now I'll play another tape for you," said Mr. Sanchez. "I made this tape last week. See if you think the band has changed. See if you think they sound better."

"The band did change!" said Lin. "I can even make out a song now."

"I knew they would get better, and I know you will, too," said Mr. Sanchez.

"I didn't think I could do it," said Dan. "But I can be good if I play the flute every day."

"I'm sure you'll get better if you keep playing," said Mr. Sanchez. "The kids in the band won't laugh at you. They know that it's hard. They had to learn to play once, too."

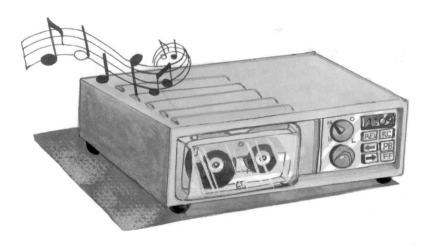

"This is so cool," Dan said later, when they were sitting with the rest of the kids. "We're going to play with the band!"

"I hope we can keep up with them," said Lin.

"You can handle it, Lin," said Jed. "No pain, no gain."

Story 5

✳ *The Newspaper* ✳

Chapter 1:
We're Bored!

Lin sat on the porch and rested her head in her hands. She was bored. So was Jed. They had been for a ride on their bicycles. They had jumped rope. They had even walked Patches up and down the sidewalk.

"We could play our sax and flute," said Jed. "We could make up some songs."

"I play my flute all the time," said Lin. "Let's do something different for a change. Think of something fun to do, Jed."

"I might think better if I eat," said Jed. "Let's see if The Pizza Pie is open. We can get pizza and shakes. Grandmother will come with us."

"I'd like some pizza," said Lin. "We can see Carlos. I bet he'd help us think of something to do."

Carlos was just cleaning up when the three
walked in. They sat down and asked for three
slices of pizza and three shakes.

"Coming right up," said Carlos. "Do you know
about Mr. Sterling's gold ring?"

"Marta said that you baked it into a pizza,"
said Lin.

"Well, it was only my first day of work," said
Carlos. "I'm glad no one ate the ring."

"Something like that would make my day," said Jed. "You and I just sit on the porch, waiting for something fun to do."

"That's true!" said Lin. "Our block is the most boring place ever!"

Lin and Jed told Carlos they couldn't think of a single fun thing to do. They were starting to get annoyed.

"We're here to ask for your help," said Jed. "We were hoping you'd help us think of something to do."

"You mean you didn't come here for my pizza?" said Carlos. "That hurts!"

"We did come for pizza," said Lin. "But we also need help. Help us think of something new to do. You're so good at that."

"Let me think," said Carlos. "I know. You can start making cards to sell. Lin can draw the pictures. Jed can write on the inside. Then you can sell them. How about that?"

"That would bore me," said Jed.

"We've been there. We've done that," said Lin. "We drew pictures and wrote cards to our pen pals."

"What's wrong with working in the lot?" asked Carlos. "You could plant more flowers."

"We've planted lots of flowers," said Jed. "We want to do something different."

"I think you're being too hard on dear Carlos," said Grandmother. "You can't turn to him to fix all of your problems."

"That's right!" said Carlos. "Look around you. There's a lot going on here. Try to look at things differently. You'll find something that's right for you to do. It's time for me to check the pizza. I'd hate for it to burn."

On the way home Lin and Jed talked about what Carlos had said. "Carlos is right," said Jed. "I've been making a big mistake. I have to look at things differently."

"You two do so many fun things," said Grandmother. "You're in the school band. You both write letters to pen pals. Why don't you write a story about those things?"

"It could be a newspaper story," said Lin.

"What do you mean, Lin?" asked Jed.

"We can write our own newspaper," said Lin. "It could be about our block. Maybe we can use the computer and printer that Carlos and Marta have. This could be great!"

Lin called all their friends to a meeting at Jed's house. When all the kids were there, Jed stood up and spoke. "Thank you for joining us," he said. "We want to start a newspaper. It will be about the people and things on our block."

"That sounds like fun," said Dan. "But it also sounds like a lot of hard work. How will we print it?"

"No problem," said Marta. "We can print as many papers as we want on our printer."

"We can work together in teams," said Jed. "We can share the work and the fun."

Dan made a list of what they could write about. It was a short list. "This is the hardest thing," Dan said. "I can't think of what to write about."

"Write about the school band," said Carlos. "People on the block would like to read about that."

"One of us can write about the horse show for the paper," said Jed. "We'll take a picture of Tasha in her cowgirl outfit for the story."

"There will be pictures?" asked Ben.

"I'll scan them into the computer," said Carlos.

"We'll put a picture with each story."

"Grandmother will help with the layout," said Jed. "This newspaper will be great!"

"This all sounds good," said Lin. "All we need now is a name for our newspaper."

"How about <u>Our Block</u>?" asked Carlos.

"It's all right," said Jed. "But let's keep thinking."

"How about <u>The Downtown News</u>?" asked Dan.

"That would be a good name," said Lin. "Only we aren't downtown."

"Let's walk around the block," said Jed. "We can think of a name for our newspaper and look for more things to write about."

"That's it!" said Lin. "<u>Around the Block</u> is a great name for our newspaper!"

Chapter 2:
Around the Block

The kids all had pens and paper. "Jed will work with Lin," Carlos said. "Dan will work with Marta. I'll work with Ben."

"We all know what we're writing," said Lin. "Let's get started!"

Marta and Dan went to find Tasha. They were writing a story on the horse show.

Carlos and Ben went to The Pizza Pie to write about the pizza with Mr. Sterling's gold ring in it. They wanted to eat some pizza, too.

Lin and Jed sat on the porch. They wanted to write about the school band. "We need a picture of us with our sax and flute," said Lin.

"We'll need another story, too," said Jed. "Three won't fill a newspaper."

"There's just one problem," said Lin. "The newspaper should be about new things. The news we're writing about is old news. Does it matter? Will people want to read old news?"

Jed scratched his head. "I never thought about that," he said. "This newspaper is a harder job than I thought it would be. People know about Carlos. They know about the horse show."

"We make so much noise when we play," said Lin. "Is it news that we're in the band?"

"Old news is good news," said Jed. "But we can write about new things going on as well. Carlos said that there's a lot going on here. We'll just have to look for a story."

"Great," said Lin. "Let's go find news."

Tasha did a spin in her cowgirl outfit. "Let's take a picture in back of the house," said Dan.

"Let's go to the park," said Tasha. "You can take my picture with the pony."

"A pony in the park?" said Marta. "That doesn't sound right. Maybe you made a mistake."

"But there is a pony," said Tasha. "There's a man giving people rides on the pony."

"We're giving pony rides to raise money for the food drive," said the man.

"May we take your picture?" asked Dan.

"I'll give Tasha a pony ride if you put a story in your paper," said the man. "That would make a great picture and help raise money."

"Our story about the band is just about done," said Lin. "We have to rewrite one part. Then we can put it on the computer."

"Let's get our sax and flute," said Jed. "Then Grandmother can take our picture."

They all went outside. Jed and Lin stood by a tree. They were holding their sax and flute. Grandmother was about to take their picture. "Wait," she said. "What do I see up in the tree?"

"It's a cat!" said Lin. "He can't get down!"

"Let's call for help," Grandmother said. "The firefighters will get him down with a ladder."

"We can write a story about how the firefighters help animals and people," said Jed. "I'll take a picture for the story."

Carlos walked into The Pizza Pie. "Mr. Sterling!" he said. "That's the biggest pizza I've ever seen!"

"I've never made a bigger pizza," said Mr. Sterling. "It's for a birthday. A lot of kids are coming here. I knew they would eat a lot, so I thought of making one big birthday pizza."

"We came to write about the gold ring in the pizza," said Ben. "But the biggest pizza ever will make a better story."

Mr. Sterling stood next to the pizza. Carlos took a picture. "I'll scan the picture into the computer," said Carlos. "It won't be hard."

"Have some pizza first," said Mr. Sterling.

"That won't be hard at all!" said Ben.

The kids met back at Jed's house. "Wait until you see what we wrote about," said Marta. "There was a man with a pony in the park. He was giving pony rides to raise money for the food drive."

"We found a cat stuck in a tree," said Jed. "The firefighters had to get him down."

"Wait until you see our story," said Ben. "Mr. Sterling made the biggest pizza ever. Even Carlos couldn't eat it all."

"That is big news," said Lin.

"It looks like we have a lot of news for our newspaper," said Carlos. "See? I told you this place was not so boring. All we had to do was look at things a little differently. When we did, we saw that there was a lot going on."

Over the next four days, the kids worked together on the newspaper. They took turns. One of them would read a story out loud to the others. Then they would rewrite parts to make them better. Lin and Jed took turns at the computer. Carlos scanned in the pictures. Grandmother helped with the layout. "This is turning out so well," said Grandmother.

"The layout looks great," said Lin. "I think the newspaper is done. When can we print it?"

"I bought some paper for the printer. We can print right now," said Carlos. "This newspaper will sell like hot cakes! If we run out, we can print more."

"Let's hope people on the block like the paper as much as we do," said Marta.

A few days later, the kids talked about how much people liked the newspaper.

"<u>Around the Block</u> was a hit," said Lin. "People on the block bought it and read it."

"Did we make any money?" Jed asked.

"The money we made will pay for the paper and pictures," said Carlos. "And there's some left over for another paper. What can we do for the next <u>Around the Block</u>?"

New Skills and Vocabulary

Story I: Pen Pals

vowel:
/är/ spelled ar in hard

consonants:
wr-

prefix:
re-

contractions:
he'd, I'd, you'd

additional skills:
add comparative endings -er, -est; break syllables between double consonants

decodable words:
card, coolest, hard, harder, hardest, letter, longer, longest, Mark, redo, rewrite, start, write, writing, wrong, wrote, yellow

sight words:
dear, different

story words:
board, person, story

New Skills and Vocabulary
Story 2: The Horse Show

vowels:
/ôr/ spelled or in horse; /ûr/ spelled ur in hurt

contractions:
I've, we've

additional skill:
add ending -ly

decodable words:
horse, hurt, loudly, quickly, short, turn, worn

sight word:
together

story word:
pony

New Skills and Vocabulary
Story 3: The Lean, Mean Pizza Machine

vowels:
/ûr/ spelled er in serve and ir in shirt

prefix:
mis-

contraction:
what's

decodable words:
misplace, mistake, serve, shirt, sir, Sterling

sight word:
open

story words:
dough, machine, sauce

New Skills and Vocabulary

Story 4: The School Band

vowel:
/əl/ spelled le in handle

vowel diphthong:
/oi/ spelled oi in join and oy in annoy

consonants:
kn-

decodable words:
annoy, handle, join, knew, noise, single

sight words:
every, four

story word:
music

Story 5: The Newspaper
Review Story

No new phonics elements or sight words